Ready or Not, Dawdle Duckling

Toni Buzzeo

illustrated by
Margaret Spengler

DIAL BOOK   EADERS

On the beach
with the sand castles sparkling,
one Mama Duck plays hide-and-seek.

One, two, three
ducklings disappear.

But the fourth little duckling
finds a friend.
"Hurry, Dawdle Duckling,
hide behind me."

"Quack! Quack! Quack!"
says Mama Duck.
"Ready or not, here I come."

Dawdle Duckling
wiggles his feathery tail.
"Now, quack, quack, Mama can't find me."

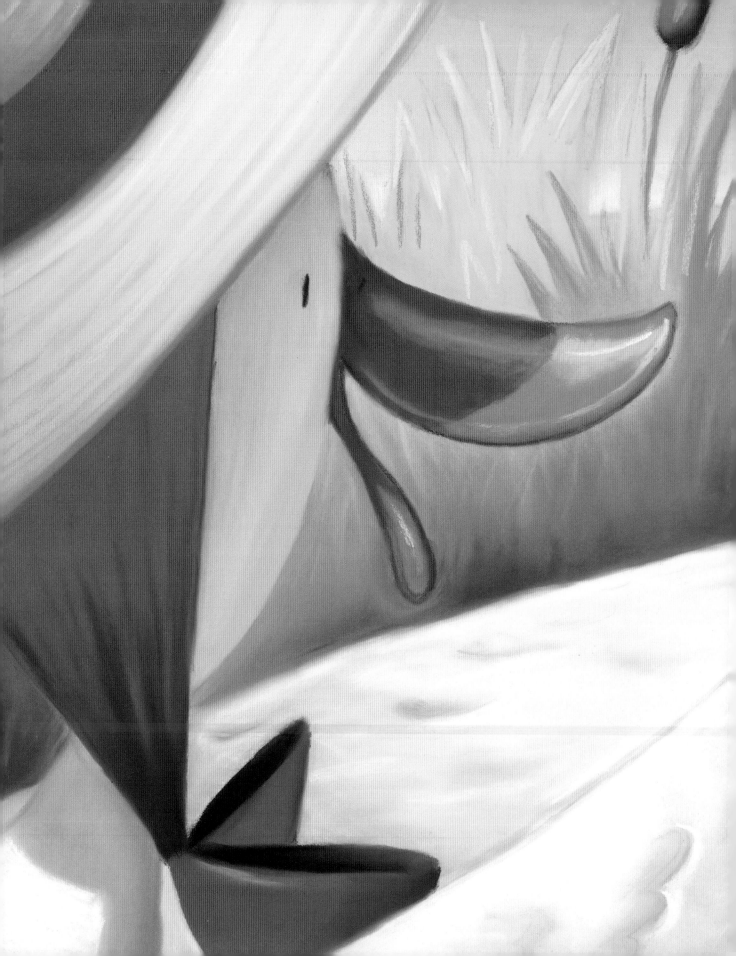

But Mama spots Dawdle's tail.
"Ollie, ollie, in free!"
One, two, three.

Around the point
in the tide pools shining,
one Mama Duck plays
hide-and-seek.
One, two, three ducklings
disappear.

But the fourth little duckling
finds a friend.
"Hurry, Dawdle Duckling,
hide behind me."

"Quack! Quack! Quack!"
says Mama Duck.
"Ready or not, here I come."

Dawdle Duckling tucks his downy wings.
"Now, quack, quack,
    Mama can't find me."

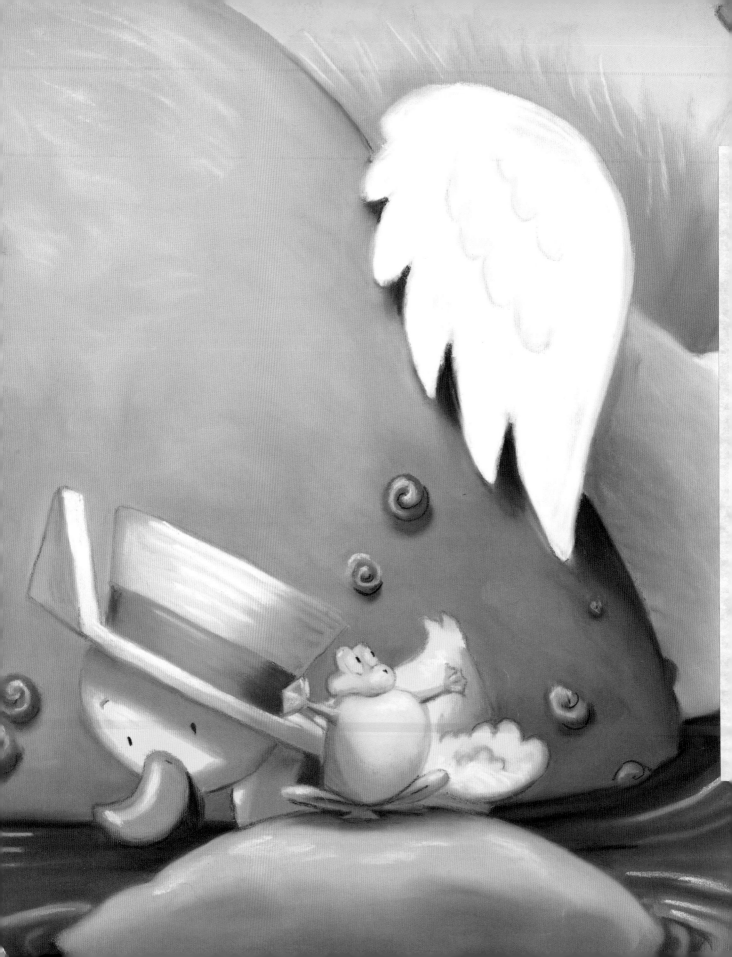

But Mama spots Dawdle's wings.
"Ollie, ollie, in free!"
One, two, three.

Across the harbor
near the fishing boats bobbing,
one Mama Duck plays hide-and-seek.
One, two, three ducklings
disappear.

But the fourth little duckling
finds a friend.
"Hurry, Dawdle Duckling,
hide behind me."

"Quack! Quack! Quack!"
says Mama Duck.
"Ready or not, here I come."

Dawdle Duckling paddles his orange feet.
"Now, quack, quack,
    Mama can't find me."

But Mama spots Dawdle's feet.
"Ollie, ollie, in free!"
One, two, three.

Up the stream
in the swamp grass waving,
one Mama Duck plays hide-and-seek.
One, two, three ducklings
disappear.

But the fourth little duckling
finds his friends.
"Hurry, Dawdle Duckling,
hide behind us."

"Quack! Quack! Quack!"
says Mama Duck.
"Ready or not, here I come."

Dawdle Duckling tucks his feathery tail,
his downy wings,
and his orange feet.
"Now, quack, quack,
Mama can't find me."

Mama Duck spots a feathery tail.

Mama Duck spots downy wings.

Mama Duck spots two orange feet.

One, two, three.

But she doesn't spot Dawdle.
"Quack! Quack! Quack!
Where can he be?"

"Ollie, ollie, in free!"
Dawdle Duckling calls.
"You didn't find me!"

To my Dawdle Duckling, Topher, who has always known the true meaning of friendship
—T.B.

To my sisters, Nancy and Marilyn, for all the memories shared
—M.S.

Published by Dial Books for Young Readers
A division of Penguin Young Readers Group, 345 Hudson Street, New York, New York 10014

Text copyright © 2005 by Toni Buzzeo
Illustrations copyright © 2005 by Margaret Spengler
All rights reserved
Designed by Teresa Kietlinski
Text set in Bookman
Manufactured in China on acid-free paper

10 9 8 7 6 5 4 3 2 1

Library of Congress Cataloging-in-Publication Data
Buzzeo, Toni.
Ready or not, Dawdle Duckling / Toni Buzzeo ; illustrated by Margaret Spengler.
        p.   cm.
Summary: After a few tries and with some help from friends, Dawdle Duckling finds
the best way to hide while playing hide-and-seek with his mother and siblings.
ISBN 0-8037-2959-6
[1. Hide-and-seek—Fiction. 2. Ducks—Fiction. 3. Animals—Fiction.] I. Spengler, Margaret, ill. II. Title.
PZ7.B9832Re 2005   [E]—dc22   2003026423

The art was created using pastels.